Sea S

Retold by

Series Advisor Professor Kimberley Reynolds

Illustrated by Victoria Assanelli

The Merman 3
The Selkie 18

OXFORD
UNIVERSITY PRESS

Letter from the Author

I grew up by the sea, in Ireland. I brought up my children by the sea, in Wales. And now I'm back in Ireland, living on a tiny island off the coast of Donegal, with my wife, my dogs, my cats and my ducks.

Island countries, like Britain and Ireland, have lots of stories about the sea. There are tales of mermen and mermaids who live beneath the waves. There are tales of selkies, who look like seals when they're swimming in the sea. But if they come ashore, and lose their seal-skins, they can never return home.

The sea is a place of beauty, but a place of great danger, too. That's why it's such a wonderful place for stories.

Malachy Doyle

The Merman
From a Scottish ballad/folk tale

One winter morning little Sylvie
was down by the water, singing to
the seals. From under the sea, a merman
spotted her.

'What a bonny lassie,' he said. 'I will take her to my home beneath the waves, and keep her there. For once the salt gets into her blood, she can never go back to land.'

The merman reached out a long, long arm. He picked Sylvie up and carried her over the sea to his island.

Sylvie's mother wept for her
lost daughter.

'Don't cry, Mother,' said Sylvie's
brother Peter. 'I will fetch her home.'

Peter sat in his little rowing boat, ready to sail the salty sea.

'Take care, my love,' said his mother. 'I've lost poor Sylvie. I don't want to lose you as well.'

Young Peter rowed, all day and all night, till he came to the merman's island. He went into a cave, then down, down, down till he came to a great palace.

Peter found Sylvie in the kitchen
of the palace, making porridge for the
merman's breakfast.

'Oh Peter!' she cried. 'I'm so happy
to see you! But you must hide before he
finds you.'

When the merman came in, Sylvie
said, 'A little fisher boy has come over the
salty sea to visit me. You won't harm him,
will you?'

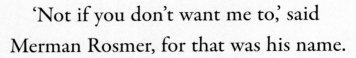

'Not if you don't want me to,' said
Merman Rosmer, for that was his name.
But he wouldn't let Peter go home.

'You must stay here, laddie, and be my
servant,' said the merman. 'For once the
salt gets into your blood, you can never go
back to land.'

But the children wanted
to go home!

One morning, Sylvie said to the merman,
'I had the saddest dream last night. The
little fisher boy's mother was crying and
crying. Please take him back to her – it is
the only thing that will make me happy.'

'Very well, for I do so want you to be happy,' said the merman. He had grown to love Sylvie, in his salt-bitter way.

'As well as taking him back, you should bring his mother a present,' the girl told him. 'But only a small one,' she added, 'for I know you're not rich.'

'I am richer than any human!' cried the merman.

He took Sylvie to his treasure room and
filled an enormous chest with gold for the
fisher boy's mother.

In the night, while the palace shook with the merman's snores, Sylvie crept back to the treasure room. She took all of the gold out of the chest and climbed inside it. Then she closed the lid and waited ...

In the morning, Merman Rosmer grabbed young Peter and the chest, and swam over the salty sea to the boy's home.

'Away and find your mother, fisher laddie,' he said, leaving them on the rocks. 'I'm off back to my beloved Sylvie.'

'Mother! Mother!' cried Peter. 'I'm home!'

The children's mother wept for joy at the sight of him.

'But what about my darling Sylvie?' she gasped. 'Did you find her?'

'I found a treasure chest ... ' said the boy. And he led her down to the rocks.

The children's mother opened the box ...
and out jumped Sylvie!

As all three hugged, they heard an angry
roar from the ocean. The children and their
mother raced away from the waves which
rushed towards them. They ran and ran,
and kept on running.

And it was as well they did. Merman Rosmer was very angry that his beloved Sylvie had escaped! He sent giant waves to smash her house, till each and every wall tumbled to the ground.

The children's mother built another home, far inland. And from that day on she, Sylvie and Peter stayed clear of the salty sea. They'd escaped before, but they might not again. For you know what they say – once the salt gets into your blood, you can never go back to land.

The Selkie

A story from the Shetland Islands

Every evening William took a walk down to the beach. He lived on an island, far out in the northern sea, and all sorts of treasures washed up on its shores.

But one night he saw an amazing sight. By the light of the midsummer moon, a group of sea-people were dancing on the sand!

When they spotted him, they ran
for their seal-skins, pulled them on and
plunged into the water.

But one wasn't quick enough. William
grabbed the seal-skin before she could
reach it.

'No!' cried the sea-maiden. 'Oh please!' she said, begging him to give it back.

But she was far more beautiful than anyone William had ever seen. And, although he knew it was unkind to keep her seal-skin, he couldn't bear to let the sea-maiden go.

'Come with me,' he said,
wrapping his coat around her.

When they arrived at his
cottage, William sat the girl by
the fire and brought her food and
drink. Then, while she was eating,
he slipped out to hide her seal-skin.

21

The selkie, for so she was, knew that she had to stay. For without her salty seal-skin, she could never return to the ocean.

She never gave up hope, though, that one day William would give it back to her. Then she could go home, to the welcoming sea.

In time, she and William were married, and in time they had three sons. They were just like any other boys, apart from the fact that each had a flap of skin, like a web, between their fingers. And another between their toes.

Every evening the sea-maiden went down to the shore. As she sang to the seals, they came in close to listen.

But she never set foot in the sea, for without her salty seal-skin she knew she couldn't last long in the frozen waters.

One morning, while William was out fishing, the sea-maiden decided to mend some broken nets.

She went to the boathouse and pulled a dusty net down from a high shelf.

But as it tumbled into her hands, she saw ...

Her seal-skin!

With a cry of joy, she held it to her face and breathed in the salt-smell of the ocean.

Then she ran home and hid it under the bed.

That evening, having fed them an excellent meal, she kissed her husband and her three fine sons.

'I'm going down to the shore,' she said.

But she didn't tell them what she was wearing under her clothes.

For she'd found her salty seal-skin, and the ocean ... the ocean was calling.

'At last!' she cried, tearing her clothes
off and plunging into the ice-cold water.
'I'm coming home!'

And every seal, from miles around,
came to join her.

Glancing back to shore, one final time,
the sea-maiden saw her husband and sons,
rushing down to the beach.

'Don't go, my bonny lass!' cried
William. 'Please don't leave us!'

But, though the sea-maiden loved them one and all, she had no choice.

'I have given you the best years of my life, dear husband,' she called out, over the waves. 'But I am a selkie, a creature of the sea – and now that the salt is back in my blood, I shall never go back to land!'

And with that, she dived beneath the
waves and was gone.

These stories come from Shetland and Orkney – the beautiful islands north of Scotland. If you ever go, watch out for selkies and mermen!

Shetland Islands

Orkney Islands

Scotland